Island of Youth

Adapted by Judy Katschke
from the script "The Island of Youth" by Becca Topol

Illustrated by Mike Wall

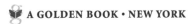

A GOLDEN BOOK • NEW YORK

rhcbooks.com
ISBN 978-0-7364-3840-7 (trade) — ISBN 978-0-7364-3841-4 (ebook)
Printed in the United States of America
10 9 8 7 6 5 4 3 2 1

Princess Elena of Avalor has many royal duties. Today she's planning her cousin Esteban's surprise birthday party!

"There will be party hats, a piñata, and a chocolate fountain," says Elena.

"And I'm going to bake Esteban's favorite cake!" Luisa adds.

"I'll play a birthday song," says Francisco.

"What about party tricks?" Elena asks.

Mateo is on it! Aiming his *tamborita* at a present, he shouts the magic word: *"Llavaluq!"*

The present floats high into the air—and then drops to the floor with a **CRASH**!

"I really need to work on that trick," Mateo sighs. But now he and Elena need to keep Esteban away from the palace while his surprise party is being set up!

Esteban is in the palace library, sulking.

"Everyone forgot my birthday," he tells his royal guard, Higgins. "Getting old is no fun. Oh, how I wish I were young again."

The library door swings open, and Elena and Mateo rush in.

"You're taking us sailing today, Esteban!" Elena says. "The royal cruiser is all packed."

"And I found this old map in my grandfather's stuff," Mateo says.

Esteban unrolls the dusty scroll. The map shows a vast
ocean dotted with islands. One island lights up like magic!
"The Island of Santulos!" Esteban gasps. "What are we
waiting for? Let's go!"

"Why do you want to go to the Island of Santalos?" Elena asks.

"There we'll find a pool of water called the **Fountain of Youth**," Esteban explains. "If you drink the water, you become younger!"

"But according to the myth," Mateo says, "the island always disappears at sundown and reappears somewhere else the next day."

Esteban doesn't care about myths—only about getting younger!

Elena, Mateo, and Esteban soon set sail for Santalos.
Before long, a brilliantly colored island comes into view.

As soon as they reach the shore, Esteban runs ahead
to find the Fountain of Youth. When he gets there, he
declares, "Farewell, old man!" and takes a huge gulp
from the pool of water. Then he takes another gulp . . .
and another.

The others finally catch up.

"Esteban!" Elena calls.

As her cousin turns to them, they can see that the Fountain of Youth is real.

"I am a young man again!" Esteban cheers.

Elena and Mateo trade worried looks. Esteban has become so young, he is a teenager!

"I'd go easy on that water," Mateo warns. "It's magical."

"You worry too much," Esteban scoffs as he fills his canteen with the special water. Then, clutching Mateo's map, he grabs a hanging vine and swings away into the jungle.

Elena and Mateo race after him.

Mateo stops running when something catches his eye. Near a waterfall is a shimmering flower growing from a bush. He watches as a baby monkey plucks a petal from the flower and pops it into his mouth. **POOF!** The baby monkey becomes a very old monkey!

Mateo can't wait to tell Elena about the magical flower. But first they must find Esteban. He runs to catch up with Elena.

They notice a boy chasing seagulls on a beach. The boy is Esteban—who's now ten years old!

"You drank too much water!" Mateo cries. "You're going to get younger and younger!"

"I didn't want to be this young," Esteban complains. "Now people will tell me what to do all the time. I want to be a grown-up again!"

Mateo tells them about the magical flower that made the monkey older. They agree to head back to find it.

Once again, Esteban runs ahead of Elena and Mateo. Luckily, they catch up in time to rescue him from a pit of sticky sap.

The dangerous journey is worth it when Esteban spots the magical flower and plucks it from the bush.

"Don't eat too much!" Elena warns.

"I'll eat as much as I want!" young Esteban shouts. He climbs to the top of a tree, where—*WHOOSH*—a gust of wind blows the flower from his hand.

The sun is beginning to set.

"If we don't get off this island soon," Mateo says, "we'll vanish along with it!"

Suddenly, Elena and Mateo hear a cry from up in the tree. Esteban's clothes are big and he is smaller—much, much smaller!

"He's a baby now?" Elena says, dismayed.

With all her strength, Elena climbs to the top of the tree to get baby Esteban. She stops his crying by singing a sweet lullaby.

The baby is calm, but Mateo is not. The island is beginning to disappear. They must leave now!

"We need to get the magical flower for Esteban," Elena says. But the wind has blown it to the top of a taller tree—too tall for them to climb.

Thankfully, there's another way. Mateo aims his *tamborita* at himself and shouts, *"Llavaluq!"* The floating spell works. Mateo rises to the top of the tree and grabs the magical flower before the tree disappears.

Elena quickly plucks a petal and feeds it to baby Esteban.

POOF! Esteban grows up.

"Why am I sucking my thumb?" he asks, confused.

But there's no time to explain. All around the island, trees and plants continue to disappear. If the friends don't leave, they will disappear, too!

As they race to the boat, Esteban loses his canteen
of magical water.

"I guess I'm old for good," he says sadly.

Elena smiles. "I like you better this age, Esteban."

The three leap into their boat just as the sun goes down
and the Island of Santalos vanishes from the sea.

"That was close," Mateo says.

Back at home, Elena, Mateo, and Esteban walk into the palace to a big . . . "SURPRISE!"

Just as Elena planned, Esteban's birthday party is full of special treats. Luisa's cake is extra yummy. Francisco and Isabel sing a great birthday song. And Mateo's magic trick is a success.

With so much love around him, Esteban no longer feels he needs a fountain of youth. He knows that growing older means growing wiser . . .

. . . and having many, many more birthday parties.
"Happy birthday, Esteban!"